MARGRET & H.A. REY'S
Curious George
Takes a Train

Illustrated in the style of H. A. Rey by Martha Weston

Houghton Mifflin Company   Boston

www.houghtonmifflinbooks.com

The text of this book is set in 17-pt. Adobe Garamond.
The illustrations are watercolor and charcoal pencil, reproduced in full color.

Library of Congress Cataloging-in-Publication data is available for this title.
ISBN 0-618-06566-0 (hardcover)
ISBN 0-618-06567-9 (paperback)

Manufactured in the United States of America
WOZ 10 9 8 7

This is George.
He was a good little monkey and always very curious.
This morning George and the man with the yellow hat were at the train station.

They were taking a trip to the country with their friend,
Mrs. Needleman. But first they had to get tickets.

Inside the station everyone was in a hurry. People rushed to buy newspapers to read and treats to eat. Then they rushed to catch their trains.

But one little boy with a brand-new toy engine was not in a hurry. Nor was the small crowd next to him. They were just standing in one spot looking up. George looked up, too.

NEW CITY	6:30 AM		OVERDALE	6:15	M 2
HILLTOP	7:00 AM		...LBURG	7:25	M 7
OVERDALE	7:15 AM		...Y CITY	7:50	M 6
SMALLBURG	7:45 AM		...IG C...	8:08	M 3
BIG CITY	8:00 AM		...TON	8:15	M 5
MIDDLETON	8:02 A...		...OWNSVILLE	8:40	M 2
OLD TOWN	8:45 AM		...HILL TOP	9:25	M 1
TOWNSVILLE	9:10 AM		OLD TOWN	9:55	M 8

A trainmaster was moving numbers and letters on a big sign.
Soon the trainmaster was called away. But his job did not look
finished. George was curious. Could he help?

George climbed up in a flash.

Then, just like the trainmaster, he picked a letter off the sign and put it in a different place.

ARRIVALS					DEPARTURES				
CITY	TIME			TRACK	CITY	TIME			TRACK
NEW CITY	6	:	30 AM	8	OVERDALE	6	:	15 AM	2
HILLTOP	7	:	00 AM	3	SMALLBURG	7	:	25 AM	7
OVERDALE	7	:	15 AM	4	NEW CITY	7	:	50 AM	6
SMALLBURG	7	:	45 AM		CITY	8	:	08 AM	3
BIG CITY	8	:	00		DLETON	8	:	15 AM	5
MIDDLETON	8	:	02 AM	1	OWNSVILLE	8	:	40 AM	2
OLD TOWN	A	:	45 AM	2	HILLTOP	9	:	25 AM	1
TOWNSVILLE	9	:	10 AM	5	OLD TOWN	9	:	55 AM	8

Next he took the number 9 and put it near a 2.
George moved more letters and more numbers.
He was glad to be such a big help.

"Hey," yelled a man from below. "I can't tell when my train leaves!"

"What track is my train on?" asked another man.

"What's that monkey doing up there?" demanded a woman. She did not sound happy.

The trainmaster did not sound happy either: "Come down from there right now!" he hollered at George.

Poor George. It's too easy for a monkey to get into trouble. But, lucky for George, it's also easy for a monkey to get out of trouble.

Right then the conductor shouted, "All aboard!"

A crowd of people rushed toward the train. George simply slid down a pole,

13

scurried over a suitcase, and squeezed with the crowd through
the gate. There he found the perfect hiding place for a monkey.

The little boy with the toy engine
also ran through the gate.

"Look, Daddy," he said, "a train!"

His father looked up. "Come back,
son," he yelled. "That's not our train!"

But it was too late. The
gate locked behind him.

The boy began to cry.

George peeked out
of his hiding place.

He saw the boy's toy
roll toward the tracks.
The boy ran after it.

This time George knew he could help.
He leaped out of his hiding place and ran
fast. George grabbed the toy engine before
the little boy came too close to the tracks.

What a close call!

When the trainmaster opened the
gate, the boy's father ran to his son.
    The boy was not crying now.
    He was playing with his new friend.

20

"So, there you are," said the trainmaster when he saw George.
"You sure made a lot of trouble on the big board!"

"Please don't be upset with him," said the boy's father.
"He saved my son."

The people on the platform agreed.
They had seen what had happened,
and they clapped and cheered.
George was a hero!

Just then the man with the yellow hat arrived with Mrs. Needleman. "It's time to go, George," he said. "Here comes our train."

"This is our train, too," the father said. The little boy was excited. "Can George ride with us?" he asked.

That sounded like a good idea to everyone. So the trainmaster asked the conductor to find them a special seat.

And he did.
Right up front.

The end.